I0654295

Constellation

By

Petar Kostadinov(2015)

Constellation

Authored by Petar Kostadinov

Published by www.pajkpublishing.com
ISBN-13: 978-0692318096 (Custom)
ISBN-10: 0692318097

©2015 by Petar Kostadinov

This is book of science fiction. Any resemblance to person, places, events, are pure coincidental.

This book is also available Kindle and in Print Paperback Copy.

Contents

Time Was Essence

"Do you recognize that eye?" He said to me "How could I? I never in my life seen such an object from the far distance."
I realized that the morning was sky dive.
But for the purpose of where I was going? That I will tell you now. I did not

have a plan. Or for the matter of what makes the sun rise each morning and the moon setting in.

I came upon this majestic sea. I looked in it and something called upon me. I don't know where it was coming from. Many times I came and swam, fish and relaxed on through out the unboring days.

My point was that I was chosen to lead something and not for myself but everyone on this Moon.

I synchronized my watch that day with the suns clock.

Something did not seem right here. It was as if

everything all of sudden
changed. Space continuum
was broken and uneven. I
might as well breathe. How
could I when everything
around me was changing.

Nobody was realizing it.
Scientists have pointed to
the weather changing do to
the life span of the moon.
The everlasting moment
that came upon it was just
remarkable. Yeah, I can say
that. But purposely or not, I
had to believe one thing.
That what we were about to
see and experience, was
mystery in itself.

Time has foretold us that
every spirited creature had
been drifting in space.

Everyone, meaning all of our loved ones, that have passed away, are there. The amazing thing about that, is we read in the bible that our souls simply live on. Yet our bones die out. It is a fact and it all made a sense now.

Why did our souls ended up here? It was as if we had been told many stories. That in a way we believed each and every day we longed to proceed the miracle.

The moment came when I had encountered my loved ones. I was not so sure what to say because they looked like my family but they

were perception of them.
Their souls, their hearts
were there. I don't believe
in any way we have had a
day in a lifetime, when
nothing ever shown up.

People of The Sun

Based on the facts we have, we kind of predicted that something has been going on out there. But what was it and why it was so bright we never knew.

One day it was on the news. That something appeared to emerge from the sun. Some kind of spaceship. Yahoo news was truthful. Sometimes people argued on there if the stuff they write if it is or not. But what we can tell now, including Area 51 and among the travels I have been with my crew, it surely proves it.

By now our technology and space boats were stronger to withstand heat. But many non believers still proclaim otherwise.

As Pointing to the Planet being Flat then Round. According to what was discovered in the late 30th Century. Everything was real. The sun had living human Aliens there. But we now finally realized. Besides the mystery that was solved, many of those non believers

still did not believe and yet
they climbed ships to visit
these planets we call home.

Neptune and beyond

I couldn't even realize,
the fact of the matter was
that I stood on this planet
and chased my dreams.
Here is the Southern
Point on Neptune. Heavy
rains, Dusty Seas.
What kind of People

would live on here? I am
guessing the survivors
would last on forever.
They have gone, each and
every one of them just
Left for better life somewhere,
on a distant other star in the
frozen time.

Bringing New Hope

Here I am now, traveling for better air and I have to bring new clear clouds out of chemicals and allergens. Asthma was number one killer on planet Earth 1, many have to breathe bad air that by time humanity reached its chorus line.

Allergens were everywhere, from cigarette smoke, factories, those with chicken and peanuts, plants, flowers, and many of which to describe them for.

I imagined clear world, where people lived free and happy. No pills, no hesitations, no anxieties, and no depressions whatsoever.

Planet Earth 1, faced many things that were uneasy on the hearts of all of us. I was send to find a cure. But by searching and asking, never had I thought I would bring out the hopeless to hopeful.

God did its miracle, and he guided me to seek like Moses,

Jesus, and the Buddha.

My greatest achievement was to heal everyone and that is what I did. The potion was created by an old man in the Third Nebula from the Fourth Sun in the 70th Galaxy.

The Much About

It was early in the morning and I had to pack up and patch up some things on my shirts and the luggage that I had with me the day I came to *planet 45*. I know there were many that forever they could be here with me.

"Are you coming?

'Yes, I am just looking

around to what I, we have come to get use to and now we have to leave to help others in the galactical realm of things'

"I know, just remember that we helped them greatly and now we have to go. I have prepared our Crew Sir. We are ready to depart as we have planned and that chart that was given to us.Our Duty has served us well here. Now we are going."

'Let me just say my Goodbyes to the People here. I will be there'

And so, we had come to sail the traveled way of life. New Dreams. New Heavens.

We Were Close to The Sun

What was that beginning
when time closed out and just
flowed into a new existence.
We were somewhere in the
universe. 3000 miles from
Planet 45. I guess the sun did

not burn us. Not a drop of rain from the Sister Moon's Rings. I imagine that every drop that falls on our ship, will be protected thousands years over and over until we meet our perfect match.

I don't know why, but this sun wasn't as its seems to be like the one from Milky Way. It was considered a Planet in this horizon.

Like Mars

I am not sure, but what Mars was and how became and where is it now, I may glimpse into this stars I am headed for now, that for every drop of rain, the forward light from the seventh sun just broken the mystery of time.

I stood there and asked the folks what has happened to the buildings of yesterday.

Old man with drifty eyes, looked at me straight and said to me "I am positive that in 50th Century on this **Planet 78** you know, there was a huge war. There was Nuclear War among the humanity with the ones that came and destroyed us more than couple of times in the early years from **Platau** and **Salou**. There was strong believe that we were the creations from their eyes. Who they were and claimed to be, was not that promised as though I had seen it before. I am very old now, been through the battles of book and the new Bible Born. But who is to say. There is only one God. The One great creation."

'I know, there is only one. Yet galaxies have planets with many other creatures and extraterrestrial human beings as such that their only mission is to take over and destroy. So, their God is somehow different or same we don't know. All we can say is that every step we take as of now, we have to protect us and the humanity out there Sir.'

"I believe so. We just need to worry. I know you came to help us. We are here every single day rebuilding our

Earth. Our crops are growing again, because we have developed this new technology that saves each seed in a special lab. It is hidden from view. When wars start and end, we have it ready to be grown in just a few seconds. Medicine we have been saving stored and ready. Our way of life, is not to be using any weapons here. We are peaceful people. How we stayed alive, is we have protected shielded homes. No Storm or Nuclear War can destroy it or us as a matter of fact."

'Yes, I see. Now can you please tell us where can we seek shelter for the night?'

"Follow me Captain. Gentleman, Ladies. Here is the first ever made Hotel. You will find great joy and relaxation to be desired for. Food; you can call the Corgiache and they will bring you something. Order anything. We have menu that contains everything from every planet in the distant Nebula, Galaxy, Planet out there. If swimming, please ring the bell when going in or out. Protection for kids."

'Thanks Sir.'

And so, we headed for sleeping. I wasn't as tired as I have thought to be. I just escaped my room for a while. Wanted to check on things.

What amazed me was that
each and every upturned
chair was glossy and
beautiful. Like someone had
just never used them. It
seems that they have polished
them.

I sat by the fire log in the
dining room. Made cup of tea.
Strong and easy on my
stomach. It gave me that
sleepy notion that I never had
before. My asthma was better.
Relaxed. I have no idea what
about all this planet. Like
great breezes took over and
cleared the air that was left
by the bad nuclear war. Could
there have been something
amazing here that we never
ever encountered before

anywhere else out there? I was just perplexed. I had no choice, but I was getting sleepy. I went in my room. Cozy and nice. Gleams of calmness. It seems the whole town and even the planet had the exact time. Nobody changed it according to where the sun had shined or hid.

The distant moon shined late that night. Every star was brighter and beautiful. You could even see Earth 1 from the distance. Very tiny dot in those clear skies.

Across The Universe

I could have been there once and many times. I flew in the spaceship with my crew.

We headed towards the Europa Moon. It was dark, dreary, nothing but the sea and the fish.

You could hear soft musical sounds from the birds in the distance.

I am just in awe. But as we known in our studies, there had not been any since the beginning of the new Cross-Incarnation back in 4598. And here we are. Something amazing is happening here. The greener grasses have started to peek. The plants have grown magnificent as golden and Godly as God had intended them to be. He painted everything right and perfect that not even one eraser must have not gone through it.

There was only old

buildings here. Few at best.
Just shelters to hide and just
find a place where storms
need to pass by.

The rain smelled as
Springtime. I could not find
any people, here.

Beyond The Stars

It was such a life. I did not ask for it but landed it. I was chosen to lead this great crew with me. We first stopped at the Glow of Pluto and their had been humans living on this small planet. Long ago they have considered it not to be existent.

Small and Blue. Jokes were created about this beauty that nobody felt was unnecessarily proven.

Orion

They called it
miracle. And it was
the sunsets that rose
above the silent
moon. I was
prompted to look
outside and seek the
yesterday to turn
every page that was
yet undisclosed.

As we
approached the
planet Turlio. It
came to mind that it
should been the
weathered storms
taking us aback. But
in midnight and
above the longetivity
of morning it was
just as swift and
sudden as we landed
on the aged old
planet. It never
seemed to amaze me
that what rose from
the grounds, was
something universal.
Something special.
Little miracle of
time. Golden gates

that were built here, and left behind, was the Work of God? It could be. For all we know, he exists and the way he created us, was without doubt the greatest treasure of all time.

I however, knew that we were somewhere new. Read many things about it in the books back on Earth 1.

Celestial Time

Build upon the sea, and
the mountains. It was created
to help those that seed the
ground. Food had been

grown so quickly and miraculously.

Every day, had its day of unreckening. Planets have discovered that rout that worked perfectly for the years that made a simple glimpse into the future.

Likewise and inventive ways.

"Tomorrow, I will go to see that light. To check in the glimpse of it in" And then it chose the sweet moment that arose of yesterday.

Short and farewell to this amazing planet. I knew that everything had been for ever.

I knew that love existed somewhere else, since it was taken away from my heart,

from the dear ones that left
undone. Because of her
leaving me and taking my
kids away, I had to start upon
my new journey to travel this
new Planets across the
Universe.

I became a captain to seek
those new remarkable stars,
that were created by God.

He knew somehow that
everyone was promised the
beginning to last.

People Of The Sea

Who were they? We questioned it. Some have seen ships come out of the seas. But then disappear in the air and back in the sea again.

I was sent to find this on a mission. For what it could been, it must have been frozen in time. There was still remnants on Mars. And we should be so remarkably proud. It was in the news all the time. Pictures with men holding a ship, carcasses of fish and frozen soldiers.

I just could not imagine what was said that some thought it was not real.

I forgotten that moment, of silence, when the reality set in. When Big NASA International Space Agency had released the truth. That were not alone in the Universe.

We never were. We were part of those people out there in space. Out of the song and into the new rising sun.

When Yesterday Sung

It had been there. The road that they built out of stones and softer layers of rocks. One by one they placed them and created this magnificent sight. But the roads were not for driving. By now, they

used hover cars as their
transportation. They used
specialized cheaper gas.

By the time we came to a
complete stop on this planet
55, we stumbled upon a sea
dust. But this one had
capability of swimming in it.
Not that dirty and clear of dirt.
The cloudy sigh of the mere
forms have me glared upon
the risen time.
I was somewhat amazed
that such a thing ever existed.
As I began to get ready to
swim, some creature came at
me and said to me "Don't go
for it"
'Why not? It seems ok and
clean'

"Not exactly. It seems but it will turn your body in mere slight non existence"
'So we shall see. My detector says it is alright. No high levels of anything'

The Day UFO and My Father

I will never forget when
my father went to be with
The Lord, Mother Mary and
Jesus her son. We stood there
next to him and waited for
him to set sail. The Chaplain
said great farewell words to
him and then he smiled for us,

letting us know, that he is in Heaven now.

I know he is an Angel now, that smile proves it all. Many times he would laugh. He held his complains and loved clean air. Helped others and learned not to be so down.

The last year of his life after the injury from Medical Motor Company, it turned worse.

We gave him help as much as we can. Stars above and now here I am this planet 88. It is great visit. Everyone that has left us, it is here. How could this be? Is it possible?

The night I was driving home, above in the skies I saw UFO. But I could not

take a picture because cars
were passing by.

I know something is out
there. And could it be, he will
be taken away there? Maybe
his soul is there and getting
him ready for the new
chapter of his life.

I know here there is no
pain and everyone is just
happy as well, they have
beautiful easy days.

At some close points I saw
my fathers heartbeat beat
again. As though he was
breathing again. But in my
true believe it was his soul,
just lifting up and holding on
to him while we were still
there. His body was cold. He
use to be warm and red when

alive. Now he was all white and cold. His body was stiff and hardened. I could not bare myself. It was something heavenly going on in front of me. My father was heavenly man. He had great energy and power in him and when I had a pain on my body, with one pat and touch it would heal me.

He went like Hemingway. Drove Medical Car like him, and wrote a book. Lived a great life. And now that The Lord took him and set him next to him, he forever knew and now knows that what mattered the most wasn't such a day of darkness but light.

When The Moon Arose

I was aware of the fact that each day I had was the sinking time. I have been on this ship for days. And what has become reality, it had to be such a daybreak.

Aware of the fact every Earthling has the power to reign among the human kindness.

When the sun came this morning, I saw the majestic hew of Planet A3698. I was not so sure if this place even had a landing place. But by looks of it, it was perfectly drawn to me, so it seemed that someone here had been living or had lived years ago.

So much desert and deserted place. As we landed, in the distance there had been a palace standing. What a majesty. It was huge and made out of stones. Made for Kings and Queens. True Royalties.

Gazing above The Sea

In mere moment and time,
it came to my understanding
that as we have stationed our
ship on Galileo, it had been
said that we would be greeted
with welcome.

I walked for many blocks.
I looked around. Stores were
deserted, library was full with
books and other media that
played on many devices like
back at home.

It seems that we have
stumbled upon a treasure.
Old world with some history.
As we walked around, we
searched for anyone,
anything, and nobody was
there yet. Miles and miles of
emptiness. As hunger strikes
our hearts, we had to find a
spot to sit and eat.

Time had shown us
otherwise as we started to
walk back to our ship. So we
had to leave it behind. We did
however planted some new

seeds of life, for the earth of Galileo could re-birth its waves of life.

To Know More About The
Author you may visit

http://www.amazon.com/Petar-K
ostadinov/e/B00IRJKJHK/ref=sr
_ntt_srch_lnk_1?qid=141759069
7&sr=1-1

http://www.petarkostadinov.webs.com/

http://pajkpublishing.com/home